EULOGY FOR A GHOST AND OTHER SOMBER INCIDENTS

EULOGY FOR A GHOST AND OTHER SOMBER INCIDENTS

Frances Webb

Strategic Book Publishing and Rights Co.

Copyright © 2021 Frances Webb. All rights reserved.

No part of this book may be reproduced or transmitted in any form or by any means, graphic, electronic, or mechanical, including photocopying, recording, taping, or by any information storage retrieval system, without the permission, in writing, of the publisher. For more information, email support@sbpra.net, Attention: Subsidiary Rights.

Strategic Book Publishing & Rights Co., LLC
USA | Singapore
www.sbpra.net

For information about special discounts for bulk purchases, please contact Strategic Book Publishing and Rights Co., Special Sales, at bookorder@sbpra.net.

ISBN: 978-1-68235-392-9

Acknowledgements

Many, many people in my life encourage me to write, too many to mention here. The primary one in putting this collection together is Aerie Webb, whose knowledge of literature in general, and whose sense of what is true to individual characters, is unsurpassed. I thank her for sharing this with me.

Table of Contents

Eulogy for a Ghost	1
We Know We Are Flawed, Poem	18
Stella Needs Protecting	19
The Grinder, Poem	28
Constant Use	29
The Sunset Is Done, Poem	37
Coincidences and Other Phenomena	38
Poem or Dream, Dream or Poem, Poem	47
Gentle, Gentle Bees	48
Just Keep Moving, Poem	61

Eulogy for a Ghost

"They're not going to give it to you, Don."

"How do you know?"

"I don't *know*, but I'm not stupid."

"But it sure is the smartest thing to do, considering ..."

"I'm telling you ... they won't."

"After all, it *was* Grandpa's."

"They won't care about that. At least wait till after... can't you just wait?"

"No." *She doesn't understand. Who knows what will happen to it if it stays where it is.*

"They probably *have* to keep it, Don. For now, anyway."

"Why? To prove it happened? It happened. No proof necessary. They didn't keep the tub, did they? When Uncle Walcot drowned in it, and this is the same thing."

"You told me they *did* keep the tub. You told me they came to your house and lifted it up, like it was a feather, you said, and carried it—four of them—like a casket, you said. And *they* said they were *keeping* it, you said. You said all that, Don."

"Don't be picky, Alice. This is different."

"Oh? A suicide is a suicide, Don."

"Yeah, but this is with a gun. Uncle Walcot was probably drunk when he got in that tub."

"Drunk? Wasn't he a teetotaler? You told me he was about to go to seminary and all."

1

"So, it had to be that he slid under when he fell asleep. And just after he gave me that little boat too. He shoulda kept his eyes open and not been so careless and paid attention to how deep the water was."

"The police sure thought it was on purpose. They didn't say … they didn't suspect no one, you said."

"Yeah. He was careless all right. Didn't care … that's careless. Well, I care. I like to hold onto the things from the family, like antiques and stuff. They get more valuable with time."

"Careless can be real, you know, Don. Like good intentions happening the wrong way."

"The worth racks up on them, like on good ole George Washington: 'Here comes George,' and they wheeled him out on that litter thing …"

"Anyway, Don, there's no way you can get the gun now, so go figure out your speech."

Alice didn't believe it could go up and up like that, just an old stupid portrait, but I told her it wasn't just an old stupid portrait. It was George Washington. "The daddy to the country," I said when five thousand was reached. So, who knows? And this gun could be worth a lot if nobody polishes it like they say not to on *Antiques Roadshow*.

"Don, did you hear me?"

And the whole house, barn really, went quiet, so quiet you coulda heard a rusty gun squeak …

"*Don!* Go upstairs and figure what you'll say!"

"Gotta at least tell the police not to shine it up. After all, I'm the one who appreciates value."

"Like they're gonna do that? Shine it up. That's a joke."

"You're right. They gotta be able to see the fingerprints. To make sure it was his own and not a murderer's. Why'd he do it, Alice?"

"Had a reason, probably."

"A reason? Holy shit, a reason to spit at everybody by making a pool of blood the size a Lake Erie and coating his grandpa's legacy with it?"

"Really, Don, your brother had a reason. Not like your Uncle Walcot who had a silver spoon in his mouth."

"Okay ... so Jim had no silver spoon. You think that's his reason? All the more reason to get something valuable back. So, like I say, Alice, I'm going down to the police station and get it."

"*Can't you wait?* The funeral hasn't even been yet. At least wait till after that. And I'm telling you, they won't give it you then either. Even if they thought you were at least showing respect and waiting a decent time. They may even *never* give it to you. Like if you'd gone down and asked for the tub back, do you think they'd given that to you?"

"I was only eight, Alice. I didn't even think of it. But you know? You got something there. That tub had feet. It was the old kind—with claws 'n toenails and all—and I bet it'd be worth a bundle now, so maybe not me, being I was only eight, but somebody. Tom, maybe, should have thought a bit about value, or even family heirloom ..."

"A tub an heirloom?"

"Anyway, Jim should of thought a bit about value and family history before he used *that* particular gun to do a dumb thing like he did. He could of at least used a cheap pistol he had lying around. Wouldn't matter if they confiscated *that* one. But this was Grandpa's ... and besides, Grandpa's probably rolling over in his grave knowing what his grandson just did with it. Not shooting rabbits, not shooting at trees, not shooting at intruders, not shooting ..."

"Stop it, Don."

"... a skunk even, but shooting *himself.* You know, that's probably a crime. It's really murder, to kill yourself. You're one of God's children too, not just everybody else. So, no matter which way you point the goddamn thing, gun, you're killing somebody. And murder is punishable by death, right? Right? Right—at least if they keep the death penalty, which they should, seeing how it's like eye for an eye ... and that's in the Bible like that."

"Yeah, the *Old* Testament, Don, not the new."

"Whatever. It's there. And if you are trying to change the subject so I don't go down to the police station, you haven't done it, 'cause I'm going."

"Over my dead body."

"Ha! You trying to be funny? You gonna kill yourself if I go?

"Don't be an ass."

"I'm not being an ass. I'm being a logical human being. So why *did* he do it anyway?"

"That eviction notice, dummy! Least that's what everybody's saying is why he did it. He was being evicted."

"Real big reason!"

"It's big if it means you won't have a roof over your head. And don't forget he hasn't paid Jane any money for the kids for a year now, so he can't be in all that good of spirits."

"Sounds like it should be Jane who's outta sorts."

"She is."

"I guess now she's *really* outta sorts, what with *no* money coming in now or ever."

"Unlike you, stupid, maybe she's even sad it happened."

"Who says I'm not sad?"

"Maybe she even has some guilt. Like maybe you should have some guilt. When did you ever ask your brother if he needed any help about anything? Not like he's so successful like you are!"

"Oh, so now it's *my* fault? My brother shoots his brains out … splashes them all over his carpet … makes a cake of blood on it, probably that Oriental Aunt Agnes gave him for a wedding present …"

"Oh, sure."

"So maybe a fake one, I don't know … but it's *my* fault?"

"I didn't say that."

"Yes, you're saying—"

"*Oh, go!* Go on down to the police station and make a *real* ass of yourself, and if they give you the gun—which they won't—why don't you—"

"Can't. They'll have unloaded it probably. Um … Hey, Alice, you think it might be a gene or something?"

"*Go!*"

* * *

Alice has no reason to react like this when all I want is my social security number. Can I help it if I didn't bring it?

"Don't tell me those cops are going to give it to you!"

"They want my license too … they're calling each Nick and Al … I got that … I don't leave home without that. That's an old ad, remember it? Now they're asking why did I want it. But I gotta give 'em my social, so hurry up. What? Say it again. One five three … two what … three … Never mind, I remember. I even remember, and I'm not the memorizing type. How 'bout that? Hey, don't hang up I might need …"

"Hey, Bud, why'd ya say ya wanted it?"

"'Cause it's Grandpa's, and it should be preserved on account of family and on account of value."

"Look, your brother might have had a gun license, but that don't cover you."

5

"Yeah, even if we *could* give it to you, which we can't."

What are they looking up in that book? Me? At least I guess that's who or what they are doing, because I'm the only guy in here. I can understand them asking for identification and all that. They don't want to give the gun to just anybody, just to the rightful owner, 'cepting I'm not, really being as it wasn't registered with anyone including Jim even—and how did he get it anyway? From Tom's collection I guess ... I mean Grandpa's. In the attic. So it being in the family and all, it being an antique, it wouldn't be registered ... unless Grandpa registered it back in eighteen ninety, but did they even have that law then? I mean, look at out West! Everybody for himself—shooting all the time. Do you think they stopped to register their guns in the middle of the desert with only a bar maybe and a whorehouse, like in those westerns?

"Huh? You talkin' to me?"

"Yeah, here's your license back."

"Um, thanks." *Took 'em long enough!* "You, um, see anything on me? In your records?" *'Cause there was that time I was stopped.*

"Yeah. A ticket. Speeding."

Whew! They can't fault you so much for that. Not like I'm a sex offender, and not like I'm out on an Amber Alert or anything.

"Look, buddy, we don't know why you want this gun back ..."

"I *told* ya."

"It's not like you are implicit or anything. Yet."

"Hey, wait a minute. What do ya mean yet? You all thinking I came in here to confess? You're thinking maybe I did it?"

"Nah, pretty obvious you didn't ... gun lying next to him, still in his hand even ... and only *his* fingerprints on it. So, you can't have done it, but your wanting the gun ... well, that's ... could be suspicious."

"I said it's an *antique*! Isn't that enough to want it? It's got value, and it belongs in the ... it was my grandpa's, and he was this—"

"We don't deal in guns as antiques, do we, Al?"

"Yeah, we ain't dealers. Heh heh."

So now they're making jokes, and this ain't no laughing matter.

"We deal with guns as guns, and we don't care if they are Charter Oaks or …"

"Hey, there's a gun for you."

"We just wanna know if a gun shot somebody. That's all."

"That's what killed Lennon. I think. A Charter Oak… Bet *that's* in a museum by now. Bet you didn't keep *that* one—talk about value. Or maybe you did, just *because* of the value, but then you would be like stealin'."

"You accusin' us? And you making light a Lennon besides?"

"No way. Just sayin' that the gun that killed the—my God, the second Messiah, peace, love and all that, and some asshole shot him, some asshole who should have turned the gun around and put the bullet in his own head like Jim did, only Jim would never have killed the Messiah—nor would Uncle Walcot for that matter. Jim was … well, I would say he was gentle-like, a man, mind you, but quiet, you know? I guess like Uncle Walcot who did the same thing. Did I tell you? He was gonna be a minister. He was going to go to seminary … wasn't there yet … still in college, majoring in philosophy, or something exotic like that. He had a room over mine up on the third floor, and he couldn't get up in the morning for his ride to the college, so my father put an alarm clock in a pail outside his door, which was supposed to greatly magnify the sound when it went off, and Uncle Walcot could never remember, I guess in his half sleep, where the alarm was and would run around his room like a crazy person. And I could hear it—looking for the damn clock—and my father laughing. I could hear him in his bedroom laughing, laughing …"

"Why don't you just stop running your mouth off and get outta here and go home and give us some goddamn peace."

"Like Lennon wanted, I know, but can you just consider maybe giving me—"

"There ain't no way in hell you're getting it back, 'cept maybe in twenty years after the record is all closed and your brother has already been eaten by rats—"

Wham!

"Okay, that's it. Grab him, Al. I got the handcuffs."

"You not gonna say my brother'll be eaten by rats, goddamn it!"

"Here … I got him. Get him in that cell."

* * *

All just because I'm looking out for our family heirlooms.

"Hey, you guys, I got a funeral I gotta go to at five. And, by the way, you guys, don't polish that gun."

"Hello, Alice? I need you to come and get me. And bring a hundred bucks."

"What? And leave your car there? You nuts?"

"No, stupid, it's the hundred bucks I need. Not your car or anything."

"Lunch is ready. Here. We're not going out. Not for sure spending a hundred bucks to do it either. And besides, the funeral is at five."

"Don't be so thick, Alice. And hurry up. My time on the phone is about up—and these damn handcuffs make it hard to hold the phone."

"What do you mean … your time on … handcuffs? Don! Are you telling me that—"

"Yeah, I'm telling you they locked me up."

"For Christ's sake, for asking for the gun? See? I told you. You don't go asking the police for the gun after you just shot somebody—"

"*I didn't—*"

"I didn't mean *you*, dummy."

"And *they* know I didn't do it, just couldn't figure why I wanted it and all, and I was about to explain the genealogy and where value really lies when this cop said he ...Jim ... would be eaten by rats before I'd be even considered as to their letting loose that gun, and I couldn't stand it, Alice, the disrespect for the dead like that, let alone *my* brother being the dead in this case. So anyway, you need to come and bail me out."

"The soup's hot—and what the hell did you *do* to get in there as a prisoner, for God's sake? Couldn't be because you just asked."

"I hit 'em."

"You hit a policeman?"

"Okay, I hit him. Just get in the goddamn car with a hundred bucks and get me outta here."

"Guess what, jerk. I'm hungry, and I'm gonna eat. I've been tired of waiting for you to get home knowing you'd never have any luck and stuff. You can rot there."

"Hey, don't hang up ... say you'll—"

Her slamming the phone is like them slamming the cell door that's still crashing in my ears, only ... only I just know she slammed—not like I could hear it. I just know she did that. Only she alone could hear the slam. Funny how that is! The phone slams down, and really the person it's being slammed on or at, or about, can't even hear the slam. To that person it's just suddenly silent. But what a loud silent it is when you know your wife has hung up on you in the middle of a sentence with no goodbye. No, "Sorry you're in jail, dear. I'll come and bail you out." At least maybe after she eats? And here he is having made his one allowed call.

* * *

"What's so valuable 'bout that gun you want it back? Don't get me wrong, you ain't getting it! But just curious. Just 'cause it's Grandpa? C'mon. So what? Besides, it don't look real special."

What can I say? I already said it all, and the longer Alice takes to come get me, the more I have to listen to these crude, insensitive cops. Maybe if I'm nice to them they'll stop it.

"Hey, cops … um … Al and … what's your name? Nice jail here. You keep it nice—clean and all—I thank you for that."

"Try this on for size, bud. I got my Grandpa's Bible, but it's just like any other Bible, and if it fell down the sewer pipe, say, you think I'd go after it just 'cause it belonged to Grandpa?"

"Seems like you might. Especially if it had his name in it or something, and maybe even your family genealogy and you could trace—"

"It didn't."

"So that did happen to you then? Your Bible went down the sewer?"

"I didn't say that, did I? I said supposin'."

"Oh. Okay."

"By the way. I didn't tell you. Yet."

"Yet?"

"Yeah, yet."

"What? Tell me what?"

"Okay, I'll tell ya. Wonder why she's takin' her sweet time coming to bail you? 'Cause she said to keep you here."

"Why? I got to be at the funeral at five o'clock."

"You got five hours."

"I'm supposed to read the Twenty-third Psalm, the Lord is my Shepherd—you know, that one. Only the King James version. I can't stand the new ones, and I can't imagine Jim can either, so he should hear the real thing. King James has got all those 'th's,' and 'eth's' on the words, and they make it like literature—

Shakespeare, you know, which it is anyway, when you think about it. Story, you know? All those miracles and Jesus being a son of God and by immaculate conception. Come on!

"Did you know Jefferson got rid of all that stuff? Did you know that? He took scissors and cut out all the crap and left the genuine and genius stuff—the sayings, the stories, or parables—I read that some place, in one of my wife's magazines that she gets zillions of, and they hang around the house forever like flies, 'cause there is no way in hell she could read every word in all those magazines, which she won't throw out till she has, and she can't. No way. And maybe I got five hours, but I gotta shave and all and read over that psalm I just told you about."

"You know what? You're a nutcase. No wonder your wife don't want you outta here. But it don't seem right to plant you here at taxpayers' expense so's your wife can have a vacation from you."

"Not my idea either. Like I said, I should be practicing the psalm. Hey, maybe you got that Bible here. You said it didn't go down the sewer, so maybe you keeping it here to be safe, and I could rehearse with you guys."

"This here is a jail, bud, not a church."

"'Cept a real church don't have walls, they say, so ... but you're right. This jail sure has walls. What I mean is, a church can be anywhere, even in a jail if you're prayin' maybe. It's all in how you view—"

"Ya know, Al? I think we can rewrite that arrest for assault and then maybe call his wife back."

"Yeah. And tell her she's *gotta* come. 'Cause you're right, Nick. He should get the hell outta here."

"What are you cops whispering about? My disrespecting God? Well, I'm not doing that. It's all his fault—my brother's I mean, not God's. It just sounded there like I was blamin' God, but that I'm not doing. I'm blamin' Jim for me being stuck here behind bars with my wife mad at me. And there's a lot a boring time I'm gonna have on my hands now she's not comin' to get me. Yet, anyway. If you don't got a Bible for me, what am I s'posed to do?"

"Maybe you could do some thinking, man, with your time. I can't stand this guy anymore, Al."

"Thinking ain't easy. It's not just shuffling ideas around in your head or getting hold of one and pounding it until it smooshes into an obsession and then goes scurrying around in a circle like a squirrel getting nowhere."

"Go on, Nick. Call his wife."

"Unless you're talking about *real* thinking, like I guess Uncle Walcot did if what he was studying was philosophy. I guess that's getting hold of ideas and keeping hold of *one* big one and nudging at it in just one place so it doesn't go in circles—sort of like counting angels on the head of a pin is what my Grandpa called what philosophers did, which I guess didn't help Uncle Walcot's self-esteem much about what he was doing in college. You calling my wife? To get me out?"

"Tell her we're forgetting the bail."

"That's good. Alice'll like that. Do you know what my grandpa did ... rather, said ... the day he found his son's body in the tub all submerged—head and all—and I guess blue by the time he was found? He said, when we all sat down to dinner and after he said grace, with some of us knowing and some of us not, like me, and I didn't know until then when my Grandpa stood at the end of the table and made this announcement, like he did a lot ... he said that—"

"Why'd you ever react to that hitting anyway and then handcuff this guy, Al?"

"You mean let that all go? Ignore that? No way!"

"Now you guys are whispering again. I don't like that. And, yeah, he made a lot of announcements, my grandpa: 'Someone is leaving a bicycle on the path where someone else is going to trip over it and kill themselves.' That kind of announcement, so I think he's going to get on me about my bicycle being in the wrong place again where it's going to kill somebody and it will be my fault, and instead ..."

"I'm gonna go take a leak. You can babysit, Nick."

"Thanks."

"... Jim was only a baby, so he never got those kind of announcements—yet, anyway—so his announcement on Uncle Walcot's suicide day was like that. Well, sort of ... just an announcement. 'Your brother, Allen (that was my dad), your son, Lucille (that's my mom), your uncle, Tom, your uncle, Don (that's me),' and like this. He went around the table, including everybody, and finally he says, 'Is no longer. He has committed the unspeakable act of taking his own life. He is on his way to hell, and we, none of us, will ever speak his name again, never in any way refer to this person who is no longer.' Then he sat down and said, 'What is this, Lucille, corn pudding?' So Uncle Walcot never had a funeral, and like I said, he'd just given me a boat."

"Shut up, will ya?"

* * *

"Hey, crackpot! Your wife is here."

"'Bout time, Alice."

"Here's your suit, Don. Make it quick."

"See this, Alice? It's a lock, and I don't have the key to it."

"Hold on, there, Mr. Roberts. Calm down. We'll let you out."

"Oh, so now my wife is here I'm Mr. Roberts, huh? Thought I was bud to you."

"And comb your hair, Don."

"I need a shower, Alice."

"Not time."

"Would have been if you'd come this morning like I asked. I haven't even practiced my part."

"Not like it's a part in a play."

"I wouldn't recite the Twenty-third Psalm in a play. What playwright is going to have a part where someone reads the Twenty-third Psalm? 'The Lord is my shepherd …' What kind of suspense is that?"

"Shut up, Don. Put your tie on, and let's go."

"How many people get dressed for their funeral in jail? Like this?"

"S'not *your* funeral, jerk. Come on."

"Yes, it is. It's my funeral that I have to perform for Uncle Walcot 'cause he didn't get one, so … Did I ever tell you, Alice, how after that Grandma creeped into my room every night looking for her son 'cause when he was my age, he had that room, remember? I thought she was a ghost."

She was confused, thinking I was being her son who was the ghost, the ghost she was looking for. So, in a sense, if she was looking for a ghost that she would see, then she had to be a ghost to see the ghost, because a ghost is only going to let itself be seen by another ghost and…

"Hey, Alice, what if I see Jim's ghost while I'm up there in the pulpit reading?"

"You are beyond belief. Get in the car."

* * *

"Did you bring a Bible?"

"No, of course not. They're in the pews."

"I can't practice once I'm in a pew."

"Oh, I forgot to tell you, Don. They've decided you should not read that, but you should just say a few words about Jim. Tom is going to read the psalm. He wanted to do that. Especially when I told him where you were and all and wouldn't have time to read it over and stuff."

"You told Tom I went to get the gun back?"

"He asked where you were and if you were ready to read, so what was I to say?"

"Geez. But he should be glad I was doing what he should of been doing. It *is* his gun. Sort of. But his or mine, we gotta get it."

"You better figure out what you're going to say before Tom calls you up to the pulpit. Or are you just going to wing it?"

"I don't have anything to say. Anyway, he'll call me to the lectern, not the pulpit. That's just for the minister, you know that."

"You better start thinking. Something about when you were kids, maybe? Since you've hardly kept up with him lately."

He was a baby ... in a cradle ... Wonder where that cradle is! Was one Grandma slept in, she told me before she lost all her marbles and—shouldn't think that—it was losing her son that made her confused. It was oak, I think, maybe cherry ... not pine ... real old. Got to be around somewhere ... over a hundred, that cradle...

"Are you coming up with something?"

That was a big mistake on Grandpa's part not to have a funeral for Uncle Walcot, especially with Uncle Walcot planning to go into the business of God, meaning part of it is doing funerals. It would of probably been Episcopalian too. Not the incense kind though. Like this isn't, this being low.

"You know, Alice, I couldn't talk about what happened. And I had all these questions, like why ... why ... and like why?"

"I told you, because the landlord came with an eviction notice, and that was just probably the last straw or something."

"No, I'm talking about Uncle Walcot. Not why Jim did it, but Uncle Walcot. I mean, he didn't even have a last straw like an eviction, 'cause he lived at home. Did I ever tell you he wrote a note to Grandpa and Grandma that said that by the time they got this note he would already be dead, and they could find him in the—"

"Stop it, Don. Uncle Walcot isn't the issue here. It's Jim. And what you are going to say about him."

"Dunno. Dunno … just that … Goddamn, why'd he have to use *that* gun?"

"Don't talk about the gun, Don, and … shhhhhhh … things are starting. Here's the minister. Pay attention. They're closing the coffin."

"Didn't notice it was open. I should of looked at him."

"We did that while you were in jail."

"Could of waited."

"Shush!"

BLESSED ARE THE DEAD WHO DIE …

"Think of something."

"I'm gonna say who's in the coffin, Jim or Uncle Walcot?"

"Cut the crap!"

"Maybe I'll say they both are."

FOR THEY REST FROM THEIR LABORS.

"Yeah. He was a baby in a cradle, a baby, when I was eight. I rocked it so he wouldn't cry."

THE LORD BE WITH YOU.

"And with thy spirit."

LET US PRAY.

Okay, Jim, help me out. I was your big brother, remember? So I punched you out a lot, and so I shut the door on your fingers—only once though, I think. So I put worms under your pillow …

THY SON OUR LORD, WHO LIVED AND REIGNED WITH THEE AND THE HOLY SPIRIT …

... but you gotta tell me what to say, you little rat, for doing yourself in. Why? Why?
... NOW AND FOREVER, AMEN!

"Tom, brother of the deceased, will read for us from Isaiah, followed by the Twenty-third Psalm, and followed by Don, also brother of the deceased. Tom?"

* * *

"... And I will dwell in the house of the Lord forever. Now my brother Don will say a few words. Don?"

"Thanks, Tom! Good morning. I mean, good afternoon ... no evening, I guess. About this time my uncle did what my brother just did, but I want to say a few words about my brother, not my uncle. Jim—that's my brother—you see, he was, well, my little brother. When he was eight and I was sixteen, I gave him the boat that Uncle Walcot had given me, and I remember he zoomed it around himself when he was taking a bath, which I had to supervise sometimes, even though he was plenty old enough to take a bath by himself.

"Like I say, I gave him his baths. I gave him my little boat so he could play in the tub ... and he should never have had a gun in his house, let alone that one. What's the matter, Alice? Excuse me, my wife's making faces at me. So, anyway, I don't know why, Jim ... You see, he was just a babe in a bathtub to me. When he's your little brother, he, like, stays that way. A kid to you, and he is maybe a dumb little brother, or maybe even a smart little brother, but either way, he doesn't die before you do, let alone make that particular thing happen on purpose, for God's sake—excuse me, for heaven's sake. If he should walk down that aisle right this minute, I would ask him why? Why? Why?"

Frances Webb

My God, there he is. That's Jim! Comin' right down the aisle. I'd better go meet him. It's okay, Jim. You are getting your funeral. Not like our uncle ... remember? Don't worry. We are saying goodbye to you. Don't worry about all these people. They're here to say goodbye to you too. Here I come. I'm comin' to meet you.

* * *

We Know We Are Flawed

We know we are flawed
Does it help to make laws?
Do they change a hurt?
Or conquer an urge
That blossoms
From a seed
Hidden in the reeds
Hidden in the veins
That with a sudden vengeance
Erupts

Stella Needs Protecting

I'm thirty-three years old. I have auburn hair, green eyes, and look like my mother, the bitch. One thing should be set straight: I am *not* Stella. My name tag says "SYLVIA" and I wear it all the time, so there's no reason to get me mixed up with Stella. My clothes have "SYLVIA" sewed into them and they come back to *me* after they've been to the laundry.

I live alone when I'm not at State Hospital, which is where I'm at now. I like living alone. It's healthful. Everything is regular. No one changes your plans. And if you feel like getting naked for Johnny Carson, no one knocks it.

Dr. Kuger wanted to see more of me. So, he put me here. Must have been a year ago. Dr. Kuger's girl? I *was* my father's girl, "Daddy's Stella." He never called me Sylvia.

It's peaceful. It's the truth I'm after, and you have to be at peace to find that. Dr. Kruger said to go to the Coroner's Office to get the truth. I wouldn't of thought to do that myself. Never did anything businesslike, official, anything with the government. Those kinds of contacts I don't have, which is why someone went with me.

They were helpful. Got me microfilms of old news clippings. "GREENSVILLE MAN KILLS SELF ONE-HALF MILE FROM PRISON." I was surprised to see that; it doesn't match the family story. That says my father killed himself on the front porch with Stella looking on. Stella couldn't of looked on if he did it a half mile from the prison, because our house is smack in the center of town, and the prison is two miles beyond Conard's Dairy Farm, and the prison and Conard's are both out on Route 15, and even if they just had got the numbers wrong but knew the right place, it still don't match, 'cause why don't they say "from Conard's Dairy Farm" instead of "from prison"? And anyway, Stella was too little to go that far. So, maybe the family has the story that way to protect Stella because the reason she's in the booby hatch is that the sight was too much for her and it got to her head.

You have to have a reason for going nuts. Otherwise, there's no excuse; it's just giving up, and then it's your own fault. But if you see your father shoot himself and you see a bucketful of blood, that's a good reason. Nobody can blame you then. Poor Stella.

Stella never made it to the home, the lucky stiff. She started acting queer right after the shooting, and my mother called the police. They're the right people to call. They know what to do, the bastards! You have to get a crazy kid out of the house. It might spread. They took her to a building with bare walls and bars on the downstairs windows. The yard had a swing and a busted seesaw. Not that I saw all that. I remember her telling me about it. Mother. She could give with the details. Cram them down you.

I have my own personal opinion about whether Stella was queer or not. To me, isn't all that queer to throw dishes down the stairs. And that mouse hanging out the window with a shoelace around its neck was nothing really, and pinching yourself till you're blue and cutting the blue out with nail scissors, that's nothing much either. I do stuff myself, so why should Stella be nuts for doing it?

I showed Dr. Kuger the news clippings and told him they didn't match the family story. He said, "Newspapers don't have the truth by the tail," and I said, "You told me to find the truth there."

"I thought it might shed some light on the situation."

"Don't talk to me like that."

"Let's discuss your father's suicide, Sylvia."

"No."

"According to your family story, it happened on your front porch, right?"

"According to the news clippings you made me get, it didn't."

"Let's pretend it happened on your front porch. What do you think might have happened?"

I can pretend anything, so I pretended for him. He wanted me to pretend I was Stella, but that was going too far, so I gave him a picture. I was standing in the living room. I was watching out the window. The paper curtains had little rips in the edges that us kids did, and I was ripping them more. I saw Stella sitting on the top step. I saw my father come around the side of the house by the wisteria bush. My brother Cal said to never eat the pods; they could kill you. My father came around and up the steps, and he touched Stella's head. He had his gun that he shot rats and squirrels with, and when he passed by Stella onto the porch, he stopped. He started towards the front door—his gun out—but he didn't go in. He turned and walked along by the window. There was this pail there to catch the rain from the roof leaks. Stella screwed her head around. I heard a bang and he fell. Blood came from his mouth. Some of it went into the pail, and some of it ran down his shirt.

Dr. Kuger thanked me for pretending. He can be nice like Dr. Welby when he wants to be.

"The newspaper's right, Dr. Kuger, so don't think you just heard the truth." But the family story is better. Stella needs protecting.

I have to know for sure though.

"Why don't you talk to your mother?"

He comes up with some wild ones.

I told Cal that's what he said, and Cal thought it was a good idea. Cal goes along with the family story. The rest of it says that my father got Josephine Tilley pregnant behind Greenley's Greenhouses, and he couldn't stand the guilt. I don't believe that. Guilt doesn't run in our family. Our family's too big to have guilt. There are too many of us—five to be exact, counting me—and counting Stella—we both got to be counted—and counting Mother, of course—she begot us all as they say in the Bible—but not counting my father, of course, he being ashes to ashes as they say there too. The clippings didn't give any reasons, but I have my own. Mother. She was unfaithful. I saw her dancing naked, and it wasn't to no television.

Dr. Kuger's right. She's the one to tell me. None of the others can. Donald's a booze hound. I never see Allen and Stella's nuts of course. There's Cal, but he was in school when it happened. Cal says he'd rather stick to the family story than try to find out from her, but he'd still go along with me trying to find out from her. Maybe we need the family story. It hangs us together. It's the only thing that does. Allen married a, you know, street person, and he never calls us because he's ashamed of her.

Today was the day to see Mother. Cal lives on the edge of the city, not far from the hospital actually. But for me to get there is complicated. First a bus to the train, then another bus, and then a three-block walk, so Cal picked me up. I have no car. Most people do nowadays, but I put my money in other things, like a television set. Dr. Welby is my favorite, next to Johnny Carson.

This morning when Cal came, that Elsie Green stuck her head out the window and shouted, "I see your boyfriend's here, Sylvia Stella."

I had my back to her, and if I could of, I'd of farted at her. I couldn't, so I turned and put my thumb on my nose. "Stop calling me Stella!" I yelled.

Cal grabbed my arm, and I got in the car. That Elsie ruined my mood though. I was in a pretty good one until then. I'm quite conscious of my moods.

"Is she coming?" I said to Cal.

"Yes."

"Did you tell her I was coming?"

"Yes."

"What did she say to that?"

"Nothing."

"Like hell she said nothing."

"Come on, sis, be nice to her."

"I'll be nice to her. She's my mother, isn't she?"

"That's what I mean."

"Okay, then what's all the fuss?" The ride shifted my mood back because the sun was shining, and when we drove in Cal's driveway, I felt excited about what I would find out.

"Did you tell her what I wanted to know?"

"Yes."

"What did she say?"

"Nothing."

"Did *you* ask her?"

"No. You can do the asking."

"Anyhow, she's coming?"

"She's here."

"She's here? Then why didn't she come with you to get me?"

"Her tea was hot."

We went in the back door. I saw her back. She was still drinking tea. When she saw me, she grabbed the edge of the cup with her mouth and hung on. Her eyes cleared Cal. After that they aimed at either him or the tea.

Cal's wife gave me a cup and said something, but I didn't hear what. His kids munched crackers and crumbed up the table. I waited for Mother to tell me what I wanted to know. She should know what I wanted to know. Cal told her what I wanted to know, so why wasn't she telling me what I wanted to know? The kids bounced around the kitchen. They knocked Mother's chair and brushed against her hair. Her hair was grey, and it shot out from the comb she had stuck in it. I thought it was auburn, like I said, like mine. Auburn. She didn't seem to mind the kids bumping into her like that.

She said nothing to me—nothing that was any help. I'll never see her again. Cal said I would, but he's not all that truthful. I won't see her formally like this morning, in a house drinking tea. We might pass at the bus station like that time two years ago when she bumped into a man because she was trying to get away from having to speak to me.

Cal sees her often. They live in the same town. He has this idea that because she's his mother he owes her something. I can't guess what for. For breeding him? Give a big thanks for that. Blood ties are important, he says. Blood separates, I tell him.

All the time Mother didn't look at me, I looked at her. "Do you know which one I am?"

"Yes." She still did not look at me.

"Which?"

"Stella."

"Hell no I'm not!"

She blushed, but it faded right away.

"Stop that," said Cal.

I don't know what Cal wanted me to stop doing, but I stopped talking. I wondered what Mother was doing at the time of the shooting. In the kitchen cooking soup bones, then she washed the porch probably, to get the blood off. And emptied the pail. Somewhere.

A month later, the authorities came to "look at our situation." By that time, Mother had replaced my father with John Ledorf. The authorities said, "Are you married?" and she said no, so they put us all in a home. Girls on one side and boys on the other. With a "no-sex" hall running down the middle. Cal and I tried to meet there after meals.

Cal gets mad at me that I blame Mother. He says she loved us and took care of us, and her husband killing himself didn't make her unfit. Or living with a man. She can still make us wear socks with our shoes in winter, he says.

I don't know myself. She let them put us in that home. She could of put up a fight if she wanted us—if she wanted us all that bad. And she let them police take Stella before, earlier, right after she dumped the pail of blood, looking like beet juice, down the sink. Of course, Stella ended up at the home with us; you can't keep a family separate like that. They'll get together … somehow.

She quit visiting. Cal said it was because we acted like we didn't want her. How were we supposed to act? A couple of times she came and sat. Was I supposed to tell her about Jenny pulling my hair two months before? The hurting was over then. Pulled so hard she had wads in her hand and hairs floating from her fingers. I already got my sympathy—such as it was—from the housemother. I didn't need it again from a lady who came and sat. And who didn't even notice the bald spot.

She could have warned me about my period. I thought my insides were dying. The housemother hunted me up and had a "little talk" because there was blood on my sheet. Her little talks were little alright, unless you had stolen silverware or written

"Mrs. Hoagland is a toad" on the bathroom wall. That was her name, Mrs. Hoagland.

"Now that you have matured, we will have to place you on the next floor with the older girls. Here are some cloths and pins. Deposit the soiled cloths in the special can for that purpose in the corner of the lavatory."

Bleeding was maturing? My father matured himself and died all in one shot.

Actually, for the times, it was a good home, if you like homes. I'd never send my kid to one. But since I have no kid, that's not much of a question. Once a week we went to the big auditorium. Girls on one side and boys on the other. The director told us how unfortunate we were 'cause we had no parents. The home loves you, loves each one of you. The home knows all about you. The home cares about you, about each one of you …

"Hey, sis, tell Mother what you want to know."

"Okay, okay, I am. I *am*," I said to Cal, him standing there like that against the sink with his spare-tire middle looking exactly like the roll edge of the sink he was leaning on. What was his hurry?

"You're fat," I said to Mother then. She was. She was blubber.

"No, I'm not. I weigh one sixty-five and not one pound more."

"You are. You're too goddamn fat."

Cal's kids knocked her elbow and made her tea spill in the saucer.

"Cut that out," I said to them.

Mother looked up then, suddenly, at me. She stared. "Are you talking to me?"

"Hell no. Why would I talk to you? I was telling those crappy kids to stop knocking into you like that."

"Were they? I didn't notice."

"You wouldn't."

She looked back at her tea.

"Did you see my father bleed?"

There was a knife on the counter, and I got up and picked it up to show her. I was only going to show her what it looked like to see blood. Cal didn't have to grab it like that, like he thought I was going to knife my own mother. God sakes, kids don't knife their parents. And then when he yanked it away like that, he practically knocked me over.

"Come on, sis," he said.

"Cut it out."

"We're going back." He took hold of my arm so hard that I thought my muscle would squeeze out.

I looked at my mother on the way to the door. Blood was running down her cheeks. What was she crying for? I never even touched her.

* * *

Frances Webb

The Grinder

Mother ground her own hamburger.
She did not have the butcher do it,
partly from integrity
and partly from insanity.

I follow the furrows with my eye
I can see the round of beef shred,
then wriggle through the tiny openings
and come out transformed …
All by the magic turning of the handle by my mother's hand.

I have the grinder.
I took a picture
(The picture is digital)
Every part is clear.
Every part is coherent.

The grinding part ebbs and swirls
In digital silence
In digital stillness.

Constant Use

I walk into a restaurant. A woman beckons to me, and I remember I am to meet her and have a dinner and go to a movie because she is in town, passing through, a common enough problem, which naturally I can attend to, the town being my resting place and only a juncture for her.

I walk to the table where she is standing and beckoning, her hand flapping like a wing. I sit down. Two women at the next table look at me. I look at them. They stop looking at me. I have power. One woman then stands up and reads the menu that is on the wall. The woman whom I am with, passing through, sits down opposite me. She is smiling. The woman reading the menu has to look over my head because my position is such as to require that. I consider her position, the position she is in, dangling over my back. Her eyes might fall onto my head, gravity being what it is. She reads. I know by that action, gravity or no, that her eyes will not fall out onto my head, because they are functioning on a horizontal level—and busy. She reads the entire menu, with the prices, to the other woman. She has trouble pronouncing "vinaigrette."

First she says, "Vin … vin," then "VinE … viniE," and finally, "VinEgret."

"What will you have, dear?" the woman I am with says. "We will decide that first. Then we will decide upon the movie. And thirdly, we will discuss your plans. You clearly cannot continue living like this. Now, what will you have, my dear."

"A ripe olive," I say. Why did I say that? It is not a whole dinner. Even an appetizer.

"I understand your flippancy to be a martini. Yes, I could take one about now too."

She picks up the bag that is next to her, which belongs to the woman who is sitting at the next table and who received the menu reading from the woman who stood dangling behind me, and then hands it to her, without looking at her and without saying, "Here is your bag," or "Your bag is bothering, me," or "Keep your bag on your side."

The woman takes it and swings it across her lap, props it against her hip and pats its side. I know she pats it in order to indicate that the bag has a right to be where it is, where it was, that the bag has a right to be.

There was a silverware bag that she, the one across from me, took from the drawer, placed the silver in, a brown and crumbled bag that she then put under her bed and gave a pat to.

"Why do you hide the silver, Mother," I asked her.

"So the robbers can't find it," she said.

"But if they do, they'll find you too."

"I will be asleep."

"Or dead."

"When you marry, dear, use your silver every day. That heightens the patina. There is a richness that happens to it with constant use."

"Now that we've decided on a martini, let's see about the movie. Caroline ... Caroline ... I'm talking to you. Stop tilting back in that chair. You'll go crashing to the floor. Can't you hear me? I want you to stop daydreaming and help me decide on this movie. Straighten your chair."

I had a constant seat at the dining table. With my back to the china closet. I tilted back in my chair. The hind legs wobbled, but I could balance. I showed her I could balance.

"Stop that. Stop that."
I thought about breaking the balance, about going back into the glass and splashing it, about going forward to the table—knocking it—about going back into the china closet, crashing the crystal gold dishes, glass bells, goblets, the tortoise shell lobster...

I feel the waitress close by. Her special problem is large knuckles, ones which make the holding of the pencil comic.

"What's so funny, dear? It's nice you're in a good mood, but tell Mother what strikes your funny bone."

"I'll have collarbone soup, please," I say to the waitress. Why did I say that?

The waitress looks at Mother. Mother says, "Two martinis." She lays a newspaper on the table over the menu. She puts her finger under a line of print. "You're the expert in movies. In fact, that seems to be about all you do."

"No, Mother. I also paint."

"And since you're the expert, tell me what's good."

"*The Lone Ranger.*"

"Caroline, please."

"*The Cardinal Sin.*"

"CAROLINE!"

"*War and Peace.*"

"That's not playing."

"Yes, it is. Look under the Napoleonic Wars, which is under N."

"I wish you'd be serious."

"I am being serious. What did you say about Napoleon once?"

"Now how would I remember that? Here's one to avoid, *Murder by Death.*"

I remember what she said. Why shouldn't she? "That's betrayal."

"Caroline, you are off on one of your tangents. Bring yourself back. We are about to have dinner. Then we are going to a movie.

So why don't we keep to that subject? How about this? *Dr. Strangelove?* That's an old one."

"You said not to worry if I fell in love with a short man, because look at Napoleon."

"I never said that."

"Yes, you did. At the top of the stairs. On your way into your room. Past the sewing machine. Over your shoulder. To me. What did you mean?"

"I never said that." Her elbow is on the table and her arm straight up from it. At the top of her arm is her hand, loose again, a flap. "Now let's get down to business, since that's settled. The things you do bring up. Did this Dr. Creature..."

"Dr. Croton?"

"Tell you to ask me that?"

"I remember. You said, 'don't worry if you fall in love with a short man, because look at Napoleon.'"

"Has this doctor of yours ever mentioned the fact of how you live? Has he ever told you that you expect too much? That in your condition the best place for you is with those who love you?"

"*Your clothes are in terrible condition, Caroline.*"

She pulled clothes out of my open drawer and threw them. A piece, a shirt, landed on the light that dangled from the ceiling, and swayed it.

"Put something on. Anything. Just don't look like you're retarded." She threw a dress in my face. "Hang that up."

She left the room. I looked at my clothes. I pulled them out in heaps. I stuffed them back in. I pulled the whole drawer out—heavy for me being seven. I carried it to the window. I lifted it onto the sill. I pushed against it and the screen fell out. The drawer fell out. It landed on the rocks. I heard the crack. The splintering. I leaned out. My clothes were in the bushes. On the branches. On the rocks. A button looked at me.

"Have you gone and fallen in love, Caroline?"

"No."

"Because that's a delusion, you know. People do it because they are lonely."

"Yes."

"Do you hear me? Because they are lonely."

"Do you remember the terrible condition my clothes were in? It was *my* room, you know."

"I don't know what you are talking about, Caroline. Stop being so contrary. Our business at hand is the movie, and I am *not* going to decide it alone."

It was *my* room after I moved to a private one, because the girl in the other bed was silent and quiet about it, under the covers. However, her eyes gave her away. I told the nurse she took my bras. That was true, but that wasn't my reason for wanting my own room. She liked my bras. They were tiny A-cups, and I don't know what she ever did with them, because she has at least a D. They would be doilies on her.

I feel the waitress. The tray is even with my head. It's wobbling. But like me she has good balance—even with her arthritis. "Do you take anything for it?"

"For what, dear?" Mother says.

Of course Mother is confused. I haven't identified the problem. "Large knuckles."

The waitress sets down our martinis.

"Thank you." Mother slides her fingers into her martini glass. She catches the olive and runs it over the edge of her glass. It slides off the edge. It lands end up between her thumb and her index finger. She puts it into her mouth. "There's your olive you ordered, heh heh." She points to my glass.

Does she want me to do the same thing? Does she want me to catch mine, too, like a fish, and eat it independent of its liquid home?

33

"Martinis are to drink," I say.

"Why, of course, dear. What else?"

I am not making my meaning clear. I perhaps should start over. At the beginning. Assume a new position. A new role. That of explainer. Which would mean learning the language again. My native language that I have inconclusively learned wrong.

"Let's have just our drink now and we'll eat after the movie. It's getting late. Drink, dear."

"And not eat the olive?"

"What movie shall it be? I want your opinion. Caroline."

"*The Room Beyond.*"

"I don't see that here. Show me."

"It's there."

"Point to it."

I plant my finger on her paper. I turn so as to bore a hole through to the tablecloth, but she puts her two main fingers on mine and lifts it off. "Where you are pointing, Caroline, is to an advertisement for computer systems. Please pay attention."

A young girl walked into my room and opened a drawer in the table by my bed. I said, "What are you looking for?"

"*People.*"

"*You won't find any in there.*"

She closed the drawer and turned her back to me. It was scarred from the treatment. I was glad I had filed my nails so there was nothing to dig with.

"Look, Caroline. See this? This is the name of the movie we will see, *Dr. Strangelove.*"

The woman at the next table who got up before and read the menu over my head, dangling in defiance of gravity, gets up and stands behind my chair. I hold my breath. I do not like her there. She begins to read. I feel better. She has her activity. She reads to her friend—mother? Friend? It is impossible to tell which.

There are no tell tales to give it away. The creases in their faces are identical: slices right down the cheeks and grooves across the foreheads. But their ages are dissolving in their martinis.

"Crumb cheesecake, kumquats—my that's unusual—something called cherries ability ..."

"Jubilee, Elsa. Want my glasses?"

"No, I can see. Let's see ..."

She reads more, and I cannot understand. They told me I had at least an eighth-grade reading level, so I should be able to read anything I had to read. My problem was identifiable, they said. It was syllables. I cannot divide words into them. I think about that a lot. Like "able." There's "a" and "ble." I can do that. It could be "ab" and "le," but it's still "able" when I read it. Whether I've broken it or not. People pass me on the street, and they look at me and they think, "She can't break words into syllables."

The woman sits down. Mother is watching them. She is watching them as she says to me, "What are your plans? Are you going to remain where you are? In that loft thing? With that girl? Or are you going to do as I suggest? And what does your teacher say about your pictures? Does she think you have talent?"

The woman gets up. She reads over my head again. "The cheesecake is one twenty-five ... the flan is a dollar fifty." She sits down.

She had no trouble. All one-syllable words: cheese—cake—flan. I pick up my drink. The olive is a marble. An eye? A red eye?

"Are you going to answer my question?"

"Which one?"

"You are so ornery. I hope you have twins just like you. What does your teacher think? That question first. Then the others. What does your teacher think? We'll start with that. Do you have talent?"

I set my glass down.

It breaks.

I hold the bowl of it in my hand, away from the stem, which sits bolt upright.

The woman across from me, my mother, says, "Oh my! What happened?"

The woman at the next table says, "flan." Then they look at me, at my glass stem.

I set the bowl back on the stem and hold it there, that way.

The woman at the next table who said "flan" says, "That's not going to mend it." She laughs at her funny remark.

Mother looks at her and laughs too. "Defective glass, of course," Mother says.

"Yes, of course."

"That's the force of creative talent," Mother says.

I take the bowl from the stem, which then looks mistaken.

The waitress comes. "What happened?"

"It broke. It just broke." Mother puts her hands out, open, like fins.

"All by itself?" The waitress takes the pieces from my hand, and I let her have them.

"Don't you want your olive, dear? Wait, let her have her olive." She picks my olive from my liquid, which the waitress is holding carefully, as carefully as she can with that disease in her fingers. Mother puts the olive on the tablecloth in front of me. "Now you can eat it."

I put my finger on it and roll it back and forth on the table. "Here. You take it." I flick it to her. It rolls onto her lap.

She looks down at it. She looks at me. Her eyes have given away the fact that it is in her crotch, red eye up, studying her like a fish unable to breathe and knowing where the fault lies.

"The movie starts at eight," she says. "We better go. May we have our check, please?" She gets up. The olive/fisheye in her crotch drops. I hear it. *Thud.*

I walk to the door while Mother pays the bill and turn and see the waitress brushing the crumbs from my side of the table. She has done something with the bowl, the stem, the liquid. I don't know what. And I don't know where the crumbs are coming from. I had nothing to eat.

The olive is by her foot. That I can see. She will no doubt step on it. I study it carefully so that it will be correct when I place it, red eye up, on the canvas, which of course is skin taut, stretched onto nails.

* * *

The Sunset Is Done

The sunset is done
It's dropped its fire
on the water
and the sole swan
swims deftly
into the firefly
flame

The moon rises
faces the dawn
and the gull
flies

Coincidences and Other Phenomena

As a young housewife, I would stand at my front window and watch the outside world. I could see a gas station, and I could see a small-frame house. I could see the garage that went with the gas station and the pumps. I could watch the Esso truck pull up to the pumps and could see the man direct the hose into the hole in the cement and smell the gas shortly after.

The gas station was owned and run by a gentle man whom I came to greatly appreciate because he would watch whichever one of my six children I had sent to the store cross a very busy street, which street, in the end, reduced the number of children in the neighborhood by two. They were not any of mine. I have to thank my mother for that. She had one cardinal rule in child rearing that I cherished. It was obedience.

The reason my children are alive today is because I took them by the hand, one by one, as they turned two, to the edge of the curb and let them, with impulsiveness and curiosity, step off of the curb. Then I yanked them back and beat the living daylights out of them.

The gentle man across the street soon realized that the child standing next to his pumps would stand there until the heavens fell unless he took the matter into his own hands. I would have, of course, eventually looked out of the window after an allotted time for a four-year old's trip to the store was up.

The gentle man had a beautiful daughter who came every day at five o'clock to help him add up the amounts on the pumps and wipe the daily dirt off of the round, red flying horse sign. He told my husband once that he had money for her to go to college, but she refused to go. I said that, if that were the case, he should sell the business and move to Antarctica where there were no red flying horse signs, and my husband said, "Huh?"

I was washing little white gloves. "If there were no pumps for her to wipe clean, there would be nothing for her to do, and she would be forced to go to college."

"She still might not want to go."

"Yes, but at least she would have to decide."

The small-frame house next to the gas station was a cleaning establishment as well as the home of a father and his four sons. At dusk, every evening, in the shadows of this dusk, the man came from behind his house carrying a large pail and walked into the shadows of the pumps and lifted the nozzles from the tanks, one by one, and pointed the nozzles, one by one, into the pail. The hose wrangled, then stayed still while the gas that remained in the hose poured, dribbled, then dripped into the pail. When he finished at the last pump, he picked up the pail and carried it—his slow walk a shadow picture against the window of the station—back to his house where he disappeared around the side.

The first time I noticed this thievery, I was burping a baby over one shoulder and patting the head of, comforting, one of the twins because the other twin had bitten a hole into her doll's elbow, and she and I both agreed that that was blood pouring out. We stopped the flow with a wad of Kleenex. It was not hard for me to enter into my children's realities. At any rate, I was shocked to see what I had seen across the street, and the next day I would, of course, tell the kind gentle man.

The next day was stormy, both in weather and in the house among the children, so the incident did not enter my mind until, again at dusk, when I stood at the window watching my oldest child make upright the blown-over corn stalks that were my husband's pride and joy and that he had planted in the front yard, instead of the back, because that way the headwinds would not get them, and I saw the man step into the shadow of a pump.

Clever, I thought, *the way he camouflages himself. Who can see him?* A giant elm blocks any views for the people in the house next door. For unobstructed viewing, I was the only one.

And then I began to put two and two together.

The two youngest of the four boys had come across the street one afternoon after we had been in the house for three or four years and asked if we wanted any cleaning done. Did we have anything for the cleaners? Suits?

"I'm Elrode, and this is my brother Donald, and we have two brothers, Clarence and Sammy, and they are football stars, and me and Donald are gonna be too."

The doll that had an injured elbow dropped onto my arm. "It won't stop bleeding."

"Oh my," I had said and picked up my skirt and stuck a wedge of it into the hole.

Elrode looked up at me with wide eyes. "We don't have no mother. So, do you have some cleaning?"

"I think I have a suit. Wait."

I pulled the wedge of skirt from the doll's elbow and went upstairs. I took a suit from Thomas's closet and went back downstairs. The twin whose doll had been injured was on Donald's back having a piggyback ride. I gave Elrode the suit and showed him a spot that I said I thought was blood, and he nodded and said he knew about blood. His father knew what to do with it. There was a special treatment, but the best thing "is washing it. You can get it out right away if you soak it in cold water and then just wash."

"But this is a suit," I had said. "I can't wash a suit. The fabric. And the shape, you know?"

"Yeah. My father knows about that."

"So, I guess I can't soak it. It needs to be dry cleaned."

"Yeah. We pick up on Monday and we deliver on Friday."

"Why don't you pick up on Friday when you deliver?"

He looked at me with confusion in his eyes and said, "C'mon, Donald. Let's go."

Donald put my twin down, and he and Elrode went off the porch, with Elrode holding the suit bundled up under his arm like a football and Donald shadowboxing alongside of him.

On that long ago Friday, the doorbell rang soon after lunch and before nap time, and I finished scraping bread crusts into the garbage and went to the door. Elrode handed me the cleaned suit, plastic-wrapped. My fingers stuck to the plastic as I lifted it up to note if the blood spot had been removed adequately. It had. I replaced and smoothed down the plastic, and peeled off my fingers. "Thanks."

"Two dollars."

"Okay." I went upstairs, carrying the suit, and pulled two dollar bills from the money jar and went back downstairs. "Here," I said, and, "Thanks."

"See you Monday."

"Okay."

"C'mon, Donald."

They walked off the porch, and I said, "Nap time."

Gradually, over the next few days, the closet began to smell—a strange smell, one that I could not place. It was familiar, but not retrievable. It might, I thought, have something to do with the spot of blood, although the spot was gone. But there was no reason for the closet to take on that new aroma.

I pulled the suit from the closet. Maybe it was cleaning fluid used with a vengeance.

I stuck my nose where I thought the spot had been. The odor was not more powerful there than anywhere else. It shrouded the whole suit. But, then again, since the spot was gone, and I was only guessing at where it had been, how did I know the exact place to put my nose?

"Why are you smelling my suit? What's the matter?" Thomas came into the room.

"Do you smell anything?"

"I haven't worn it. I don't know."

"They got the blood out."

"Good."

"I could have gotten it out with cold water. Myself. By soaking. Don't you smell something?" I held up the plastic and positioned the suit in front of my husband so he could smell.

"Yes. Gas."

"Of course. That's it. That's why he—I mean the father—stole from that sweet man. Do we keep getting our cleaning done there knowing this?"

"Not if I am going to smell like a gas tank."

"I'll air it out."

"Fine."

So, I continued to patronize Elrode and Donald, figuring I could always air out the suit, and each of my children, in turn, got piggyback rides. Elrode and I got so that we shook hands over our transactions. Once I asked him if his two older brothers worked as hard as he and Donald did, because it was clear that the family needed money.

"Yeah," he said, "they play football."

"No, I mean employment."

"Employment?"

"That's right. Earn money."

"Yeah. Sammy teaches moves."

"Moves?"

"Yeah. Football moves. You know, strategies. See you Friday."

He left with his bundle, and Donald said, "No more rides, kids. See you Friday," and he punched his arms into the air, walking alongside Elrode.

On Friday they brought the clothes, dragging the extra plastic along the sidewalk, and when I met them at the door, I noticed a puzzled look on Elrode's face. "What is it?" I asked him, not wanting anything to interfere with our goodwill, and he said, "What's your husband doing at night out here in those corn stalks?" and he waved his arm in the direction of the front field.

"Why do you ask? What do you see?"

"Shooting, that's what I see, and I hear it. We all hear it, so I come over, and I look, and he's shooting, and corn is going in the air like the Fourth of July. What's he doing that for?"

"Target practice, Elrode. That's all. Target practice."

"Corn?"

"It's as good as anything, isn't it?"

"Yeah, I s'pose. But out here? In the front? By the street?"

"He has perfect aim. And it's thanks to those small burgeoning ears of corn."

"I thought you eat all that corn you grow."

"We do, but there's always some that gets too old."

"I thought you said he hits the small ones."

"The small ones sometimes get old before their time."

"Oh. Here's your clothes."

"Thanks."

Now that they knew our little secret, I began to watch more closely the activities across the street. Clearly, we were going to have a competition of secrets.

Gas wasn't the only thievery, it turned out.

The kind, gentle man, I noticed, was gone by sunset. The beautiful daughter, though, was not, or if she was, she came back. Because there she was as I stood by the window dealing with the squabble behind me, unlocking the padlock that her father had locked a half hour earlier on the garage door. And there she was leaning over the garage door, her skirt rising like a lilac in the breeze, and the backs of her thighs shining like white turnips. The garage door rose and rode back on its trestle, leaving a gaping dark hole.

Either Sammy or Clarence—since I had never seen them, I did not know which was which, but I knew it was one or the other because whichever one it was came from the same dusky shadow as the man with the pail—walked toward the gaping hole. She, to one side standing now, turned and looked and unbuttoned her blouse. He stepped toward her, and she let go of the rope that held the door up, and the door came down. The only thing I could see then that was in any part connected to the two of them was a piece of that blouse sticking out beneath the door.

I thought of our good fortune as compared with the other part of society across the street, and I said to Thomas, who was behind me now, preparing his nightly game with the children, "You never thought you'd have six, did you?"

"No."

"With six, if one goes wacky, it's not so bad, right?"

"Yes, there are the other five."

"But what if two go wacky?"

"At least there are four."

"And three?"

"Get off it. What are you trying to do?"

"Be logical."

"Bedtime, children!" Thomas gathered them together and sat them on the edge of the carpet. He made sure they were way to the edge, far from the center. Then he laid his long rifle in the center of the rug. He drew coins from his pocket. He spread the coins on the swirls of roses in the center of the carpet and picked out a nickel. He picked it up, then gathered the other coins and returned them to his pocket.

"All right everybody, here we go." He threw the nickel into the center (onto the center) of the rug and said, "Now, tell me. What time is it?"

One of the children looked at the clock and said, "Seven thirty," and my husband said, "No, no, no! You know the game. From the coin. Tell from the coin on the rug. It's placement."

The oldest got up and studied the situation.

"I'll give you a hint." My husband picked up the rifle and aimed it at the nickel. The shot splintered the air and sent each child bobbing on its haunches, like a series of amusement park ducks, and the silver remains of the nickel flowered into the air.

My oldest shouted above the hubbub, "Bedtime! Right, Dad? You mean the time is *bedtime*."

Of course, this was not the first time the game had been played, so she, and the others if they had been paying attention the other times, had certainly an inkling.

"*Right!*" said Thomas.

That oldest ran for the stairs. The others, like pied piper children, followed her. Thomas grinned, and I got out the vacuum cleaner, plugged in the chord, aimed the nozzle at the small fragments of wood and silver, and sucked them into the round belly of the Electrolux.

And with wood putty, which I had ready, I plugged up the hole in the floor.

We both went upstairs then to kiss the children good night.

As a young housewife, I was content to watch the outside world and not be a part of its thievings, tits for tats, secrets, and other goings on. Now, as an old housewife, gray and full of fluid, I think sometimes about that gentle man across the street who kept my children alive and who had to live with such disappointment in his one beautiful daughter with thighs of white turnips, fleshy and firm, who knew to keep the rope of the garage door taut until the appropriate moment to let go.

That certainly was not something I would have ever been able to do.

* * *

Poem or Dream, Dream or Poem

a band is playing in the distance ...... *dream*
poem ...... under elms
so faded
dream
in the shade

poem ...... drums: timpani, snare
loud fast allegro
dream
then a sound from ... from ... where?

d
nowhere near
r
afar, above, beyond,
e
the words not even clear:
m

NO! Not right! Not the original!
dream
Play that: play the original!

So the music slowed.
It lost crescendo
then silenced ... no!
poem ... dream
It still played—
slow, muted,
scared?
poem/dream/the difference is ...

Gentle, Gentle Bees

Georgina and I met on the street by my front gate. She was just about in front of it, and I was coming from the house toward it. Our "hellos" were almost simultaneous.

She had one child by the hand. I had one child by the hand. Hers was a girl. Mine was likewise. Hers had a ponytail. Mine had two pigtails. We both asked at the same time: "How old is your little girl?"

"Four."

"What's her name?"

"Karen. What's hers?"

"Susan. Susan this is Karen. Say hello to Karen."

Susan didn't.

"Karen, this is Susan. Say hello to Susan." Karen didn't.

They picked at the paint on the fence and peered at each other through the pickets. We, as mothers, watched them and also watched our hands that were placed on the picket tops of the gate. Georgina had long, long fingers, and the ends of them dangled over the edge of the picket tops. My fingers were short, stubby, not capable of dangling.

"My name is Georgina. I, we, live up the hill. The house with the beehives."

"I hadn't noticed a house with beehives. I'm Elizabeth."

"The hives are in the back."

"I guess that's why I didn't notice them."

"Jars of honey are on a table in the front. I sell it."

"Oh. I did see the honey. I thought it was to attract Japanese beetles. I usually use beer for that. They love it. They take one drink and drop in and that's the end. They drown in the beer. What a way to go!"

"It would be kind of hard to drown in honey. Anyway, there are tops on my jars. The honey is not there for gardening purposes."

"It *would* be kind of hard to drown in honey ... sticky."

"I charge quite a bit. So, it's selective, when you think about it, whom I sell it to."

"Of course."

"But, naturally, the price depends on how much is produced." She took her hands from the gate.

I took my hands from the gate also.

Karen ran between my legs and the gate. Susan ran between Georgina's legs and the gate. They ran along their respective sides of the fence all the way to the corner. Once there, Karen nestled herself into the fence corner and placed her hands in the slits between the pickets. Susan stood on the outside of the corner, and the line of the outer edge of the corner lined her body from her chin to her toes. She put her hands in the slits also, the same slits so that they landed on top of Karen's hands, sideways, up and down. Georgina and I watched this and waited for the next move. I was surprised, and I guess Georgina was too, by what it was. They moved their faces close to the fence, put them against the slit between the one holding their hands, and rubbed noses.

Leonard and I received an invitation then, not long after that, and we went, in the evening, to visit Georgina and her husband.

"Come in," she said as she opened the door after our steady, long, long ring. "Jake and I have been discussing which chairs you would like to sit on. You have your choice. I shall sit here."

She sat on the love seat and crossed her knees. "Now we can get to know each other. Better. Without husbands. Since Elizabeth and I have already had an initial get-acquainted chat, we will wait for you two men to catch up to us, won't we, Elizabeth?"

"Yes," I said. Leonard and I still had not sat down. We looked at the four chairs from which to choose. We did not look at each other. It was not one of those decisions that married people make as a mutual consensus. He sat. I then had three to pick from.

"Sit, love," Georgina said, and the command caused me to turn on the exact spot where I was standing and sit on the chair that happened to be exactly behind me. Which was directly opposite Georgina, so I looked at her directly and not at an angle. And, as I looked, I saw her eyelids move slowly down over her eyeballs. They flung up immediately. Her head gave way inch by inch, though, and I could see the long hair part down the middle of her head. She uncrossed her legs and lay down on the short love seat with her knees drawn up in a baby-like position, then put her hands, one on top of the other, under her cheek and went finally and completely to sleep.

Our husbands zipped up the virgin conversation, then remembered, evidently, their assignment, so they opened another one, carried it along. It was about cows.

I knew nothing about cows. Other than the obvious function that they perform: to milk the nation, and if not that, then to be beef.

Georgina was definitely leadenly asleep. The men continued about cows. Where they graze and what it does to the milk.

I said, "What about fallout?"

"That's an issue too," Georgina's husband said. He was looking at Georgina. He needn't. Leonard and I weren't upset at her sleeping, but we did need to keep things going, both for the husbands' sakes and for mine, even though I had not been included in the assignment. My reason had to do with being uncomfortable with silence.

Georgina stirred.

She was, perhaps, waking up? Maybe? No. She settled herself. And snored.

The fallout issue was waning, so I hunted for an offering. The bees. "How are the bees?" I looked at Jake.

"How did you know about the bees?" he said.

"The honey outside."

Georgina's mouth was hanging open.

"Yes, it's for sale. Georgina's pin money."

"Does she take care of them?"

"Yes, naturally. They are her ..."

"Bee babies?"

Georgina suddenly sat up. "We have too many hives standing around empty. Only two are inhabited. Mr. Carr paid me an official visit. He was working up statistics for the state." She lay back down, but her mouth, open from talking, stayed open.

I looked at Jake. He was making the tips of his fingers meet and was watching them meet. I looked at Georgina. She was dreaming, having invited us, dreaming.

Her mouth shut. Closed, it was a long, thin line that looked penciled onto her face.

Again, she sat up. "The hive I tried to produce by division he pronounced too weak to even try to keep. I followed his instructions and emptied it into one of the others. We need to be in a profitable bee locality. We aren't." She lay back down.

"Is that true?" I asked Jake, not because I care but just to keep things rolling along.

"Well, yes. We have the field, but it's not nearly big enough. If their area isn't big enough, they have to work too hard to get pollen, and then Georgina ends up with tired bees."

She sat up. "We could produce eighty pounds a year."

She lay down. Soon she was snoring again, an in and out puffing. Messages from herself to herself?

Jake and Leonard discussed fields, the proper and improper kind.

I watched Georgina pull her hands from under her cheek and let one drop, loose, by the side of the love seat. I wondered if her therapist, whom I assumed she must have, knew she slept through her act as hostess. I can tell by my use of the word "act" that I was beginning to get annoyed at her sleeping, since we had been invited. We had not merely dropped in.

She was stirring. Hearing an alarm in her head, perhaps: "I invited these people. I should wake up and talk to them."

She sat up. "Shall I continue?"

"By all means," I said.

"He told me that probably the reason I lost so many hives last winter was that there was no protection under the hive floor. I should have put the hives on blocks and packed leaves underneath and around. I should have done that at the first frost. I didn't."

She lay down. No, she was up. "I have done that now, and the bees fly as if they felt warm." Down she went.

"She seems to take the raising of bees very seriously," I said to Jake. "She talks about them as though they were her babies."

"It's her life."

"If they are her babies, then I guess it is her life. Do they ever sting her? Does she ever get stung?"

"No. I see you have the usual misconception about bees. They don't sting for the hell of it. Willy-nilly. They sting out of fear, which happens if they lose empathy with the keeper." He looked at Georgina. "It would do no good to wake her. I will wake her to get her upstairs, but that will be only a motor reaction."

She lifted her head. "There are just two hives to go over the winter now that I have given Mr. Carr one, and they are real strong. Also, he told me to remove the excluder and leave the super on. There is not much honey in that, he said."

"Is there really an official inspector?"

"She's dreaming. She's dreaming."

She sat up. "The stinging fluid, the juice of the bee, by the way, is the milk of the colony. That is to be understood by those in charge of the land of milk and honey." She lay down.

I smiled and looked at Jake.

He smiled too. "When it comes to dreams ..."

She sat up. "Here is a partial report on the bee business. The state bee inspector told me what the price should be. I have sold half of what I extracted. I have done no advertising." She lay down.

She may have done no advertising, but what did she think jars of honey on a table on the front lawn were? However, she was right. There was no price on the jars. That would leave people guessing. Leave people wondering about the intent of the jars on the table—as I did, thinking that there were there to catch beetles unawares, not taking note, as I certainly should have, that there were tops on the jars.

It was quiet in the room. Jake and Leonard were silent. Done their assignment. Jake was interlacing the fingers of his hands, and Leonard was rubbing his thumb on the ice in his glass. I was responsible for their being thrown into this predicament, since I had become Georgina's friend. I was therefore responsible for getting them out of it. Georgina was certainly in no shape to take on that burden.

I looked at my watch and said, "My, I had no idea it was so late. The time has simply flown."

Leonard jumped up. "Yes, I have an early day tomorrow."

Jake unlaced his fingers and got up. "My pleasure."

"Shall I ... would you like ... do you need ..." Leonard nodded toward the love seat.

"No, no. I can get her upstairs. She'll wake up enough to move her legs."

"Does she do this often?"

"No. Not like this. But she's an unusual woman. One never knows."

"Seems odd." Leonard looked at me. I assumed for agreement. I gave none. Instead, I waved to Georgina. Both men looked at her to see if my wave clubbed her into wakefulness.

She did not move.

Leonard then quickly turned to me. "Remember the company picnic, Elizabeth? Remember how you are allergic to bees. They're not your cup of tea."

"Don't worry. I won't have tea with them." Unless I'm invited.

From her prone position, and with her eyes closed, Georgina said, "The bee, my dears, is any hymenopterous insect of the super-family *Apoidea*."

As we headed for the door, I wondered if she fell asleep over her hymenopterous insects *Apoidea* as well as over her *homo sapien* friends.

The next morning as I was buttoning Karen's coat to take her on a stroll, the phone rang. It was Georgina. I should have been the one to call her since I had been the guest at her house, even if an unwanted one, so I immediately said, "We enjoyed last night very much."

"How could you have?"

The question took me by surprise, but I recovered and said, "I understood. You were tired."

"No, I wasn't."

"Your husband. He's interesting."

"Was he?"

"Jake and Leonard seemed to hit it off."

"Maybe. But they put up with each other because of us."

The "because of us" made my heart pound. Maybe she had wanted to stay awake and couldn't help it.

"Would you like to see my bees? I am going to extract the honey today."

"Oh yes, yes."

"Bring Karen."

"Of course." How could I not bring Karen? I could not leave her alone, napping, asleep in her room.

"Has she ever seen how bees live?"

"No."

"Good. This will be an experience for her. Susan was initiated early. We took her to my uncle's. He had a hive in his house, right in his house, in the walls, and instead of exterminating, he glassed it in, made it a showplace. We sat in his living room and watched, watched everything, the whole life of them."

I wanted to ask her if she had managed to stay awake in her uncle's living room, but I *had* sort of forgiven her with the "because of us," so I didn't.

"Susan put her nose up to the glass and watched and watched. It was like the bees had incorporated that glass into their community—adapted—as though they were thanking Uncle Davis for not doing them in. When I take Susan to my hives here, she knows, of course, that there is no glass, and she knows exactly where to stand. Do you think Karen would stand with Susan? Would she stand still with Susan?"

"If I tell her she has to, she will."

"She won't run to the bees? To see them? Up close?"

"Not unless she has a reason to."

"Are you saying that Susan will give her a reason to?"

"No, of course not. I'm saying that if she sees a dog, or cat, or bird, or squirrel, or … But if I tell her that she is not to move, even if she sees a dog, or cat, or bird, or squirrel …"

"You'd better think of every possibility. It sounds like she will run to a python unless you say, 'Don't run to a python.'"

"No, she has some sense."

"I hope so. You can come now if you want. I am headed down to the bees in a few minutes."

"By the way, do you have your bees inspected?"

"What do you mean?"

"Last night. You kept talking about Mr. Carr and the inspector."

"I did?"

"Yes."

"I don't remember. I'll see you in a few minutes."

I guessed I would not know if the bees got inspected or not. I finished buttoning Karen's coat, who by then had gotten started with a doll, leaving her coat flapping and her hat on backwards. "Come, Karen," I said. "We are going to see some bees."

"Why?"

"It's interesting."

"I know why you want to go. You want to catch the bee that stung you at the picnic and then kill it."

"No, no. That is certainly not my plan. I want you to see how bees live. I'm not looking for that bee."

"You should. You should kill it. It made you ugly. You looked like a monkey."

"Yes, I know I did."

"Why do you want to look like a monkey again?"

"I don't."

"Then why are we going to see bees?"

"I'm not going to get stung, Karen. We are going to look at how they live."

"They live for stinging."

"No, they live to make honey. That is their job. To make the world sweet."

"They sting. I don't want to go."

"They only sting when the empathy is broken between them and their keeper."

She was back with the doll, and I had to pry her loose from it. She screamed. I tried to take the doll away, it being past the time to leave, but every time I got one of her fingers loose from the doll, she tightened with another.

"Come, Karen!"

She screamed.

I screamed back, "Do you want the bees to sting your doll?"

She let go. I put the doll on the couch. I took her hand. She took mine. We went out the front door, through the gate, and up the street.

"Hurry." I was afraid Georgina would have left for the hives.

I rang the doorbell.

The door flung open and Susan said, "Mommy said come in."

Karen would not let go of my hand. "Play with Susan while we wait," I said. But she would not let go of me. "What's the matter with you?" I pried her hand loose.

Susan stood in front of her and stared. Finally she said, "Did you forget me?"

Karen shook her head no.

Susan went to the foot of the stairs. "Mommy, they are here, and Karen is stuck to Mrs. Promise!"

"You can call me Aunt Elizabeth," I said.

"I'll be down in a minute," called Georgina.

Susan came back and stared at Karen again.

"I am *not* stuck to her."

"Then let go," Susan answered.

Georgina came downstairs.

"I will." Karen let go and, without looking at me, followed Susan out the door.

I was proud of the way I had handled the situation.

Georgina walked over to me. She kissed me and gave me a hug. We split apart, and I said, "Where did Karen and Susan go?"

"They went outside."

"What are they doing?"

She walked to the door. Looked out. Came back toward me. "They are sitting on the step."

"I knew they were all right," I said.

"No, you didn't." She came closer to me and put her hands on my face. "You must be more honest. You will suffer less."

"I don't suffer."

"Yes, you do. That is how you suffer. By not suffering."

We walked down the path away from the house. Ahead of us was a large field. Yellow and blue flowers dotted the top of the field. Karen and Susan skipped ahead of us, holding hands. Once they stopped and hugged.

"How far are the bees?"

"Another few hundred yards. Down that hill." Georgina had a long, thick, yellow garden glove in each hand. She swung them. Rhythmically. They looked like golden fingers.

"I should tell you," I said. "I'm allergic to bees."

"I know that."

"How did you know that?"

"Your husband reminded you of that fact when you were leaving my house last night."

"You were asleep."

"Yes, that's right."

"Then how...?"

"Don't worry. We're almost there."
"But you don't remember talking about a bee inspector?"
"No."
"And the family that bees are in?"
"No."
"And their care, their needs?"
"No."
"This is preposterous."
"Yes." She walked ahead of me then, ending the conversation. I called after her, though, to "be sure to stay awake." I cupped my hands around my mouth and repeated my warning, but she kept walking.

The hives were near, and I could see small, quick, yellow movements. She placed Susan and Karen off to the left.

"Can they see?" I called.

"Be quiet," she said with her lips—no sound—but I knew what she said. She was leaning over the children, and they were nodding. She stood up and went toward the hives, putting on her gloves as she walked.

I remembered the list for Karen and turned and went over to her. "Don't move," I said to her, "even if you see a dog, a cat, a bird, a squirrel …"

"Look, she's opening the door," Susan whispered. "She's going to get a honeycomb. And we can suck the honey."

"Oh, goody goody!" Karen hugged Susan, then grabbed her hand.

Karen was not listening to me at all.

I straightened up. She *had* to. I needed to make her listen.

I could hear a buzzing and a whispering. Georgina was talking to the bees. They *were* her babies.

"Karen," I called, "not even if you see a python!"

"What's that, Mommy?" She dropped Susan's hand.

"A snake ... never mind *what it is*, just don't move."

"Where's the snake, Mommy?"

"Nowhere."

"I want to see the snake! I want to see the bees!" She jumped and ran ahead of where Susan was still standing still, and of where I was standing still, and down toward Georgina and toward the hives.

"No, Karen!" yelled Susan.

"Come back, Karen!" I yelled.

Georgina pulled her right arm from the hive. Bees covered it. More flowed from the hive. She pushed my Karen with her left arm. Karen fell back, got up, and ran back to Susan. Bees left the hive and became an umbrella. A long, yellow glove reached toward them, then they became a black and yellow wool coat, and I wondered if there was anything I should do about what was happening to Georgina—if I should do anything to get the honey out of the hive—but I really knew nothing about bees. I hunted and hunted for something to say, but all I could think of was to ask her if the inspector was due.

* * *

Just Keep Moving

Just keep moving!
That is the answer to all of life!

Cross the bridge no matter no sides or how narrow
Hang-glide the world below; you will move with it.
Climb the rock wall no matter how harrowing
Swim the river of sharks; the teeth will miss your toes and fingers.
Walk through dark mazes; you will come out at the end
Count the stars that sneak through the clouds and linger.
Think through those mathematical jungles
You won't stay tangled
Just keep moving and not crumble
The answers may be mangled
Or not even there
But no matter the stumble
PI lives forever forever forever, here or there

Just
Start
Early
And keep moving

Review Requested:

We'd like to know if you enjoyed the book.
Please consider leaving a review on the platform
from which you purchased the book.

CPSIA information can be obtained
at www.ICGtesting.com
Printed in the USA
BVHW071831030521
605996BV00001B/1/J